A JUST ONE MORE BOOK
Just For You

# The Pup Went Up

by Mary Blocksma

Illustrated by Sandra Cox Kalthoff

Developed by The Hampton-Brown Company, Inc.

 CHILDRENS PRESS, CHICAGO

# Word List

Give children books they can read by themselves, and they'll always ask for JUST ONE MORE. This book is written with 67 of the most basic words in our language, all repeated in an appealing rhythm and rhyme.

| | | | |
|---|---|---|---|
| a | get | make | said | up |
| about | go | me | see | |
| all | goat | more | sheep | very |
| and | got | my | snake | |
| at | | | so | want |
| | help | next | some | what |
| blue | hens | no | | we |
| boat | hop | | take | went |
| by | | off | ten | will |
| | I | on | the | with |
| cake | in | one | there | |
| can | is | | they | you |
| coat | it | paint | this | your |
| | | pup | three | |
| down | just | | to | |
| | | ran | town | |
| floor | last | red | two | |
| for | | room | | |

Library of Congress Cataloging in Publication Data

Blocksma, Mary.
   The pup went up.

   (Just one more)
   SUMMARY: A pup on an elevator adds various animals along the way as he ascends to the very last floor.
   [1. Stories in rhyme.   2. Animals—Fiction]
I. Kalthoff, Sandra Cox, ill.   II. Title.
PZ8.3.B5983Pu   1983      [E]      82–19862
ISBN 0–516–01583–4

The pup went up.

Up went the pup and up some more.

3

A goat got on at the very next floor.

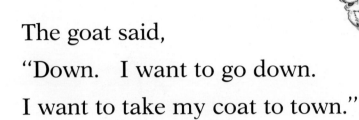

The goat said,

"Down.   I want to go down.

I want to take my coat to town."

"Go up," said the pup.

"Go up with me.

My boat is up there.   You will see."

So a goat in a coat and the pup went up.

Up they went and up some more.

Two sheep got on at the very next floor.

The sheep said,
"Down.   We want to go down.
We want to paint some blue in town."

"Go up," said the pup.
"Go up with me.
My boat is up there.   You will see."

9

So two blue sheep, a goat in a coat, and the pup went up.

Up they went and up some more.

A snake got on at the very next floor.

The snake said,

"Down.　I want to go down.

I want to take my cake to town."

"Go up," said the pup.

"Go up with me.

My boat is up there.　You will see."

So a snake with a cake, and two blue sheep,
a goat in a coat, and the pup went up.

Up they went and up some more.
Ten hens will get on at the very next floor!

"No room!" said the sheep.

"No room!" said the snake.

"No room!" said the goat.

"No room!" said the cake.

"Get up,"
said the pup.
"Get up on me.
We can make it.   You will see."

So ten red hens, a snake with a cake,
two blue sheep, a goat in a coat,
and the pup went up.

Up they went and up some more.
They all got off
at the very last floor.

The snake and the sheep,
ten hens, and the goat
ran by the pup to get in the boat.

In they went—one, two, three.

"Help!" said the pup.

"What about me?"

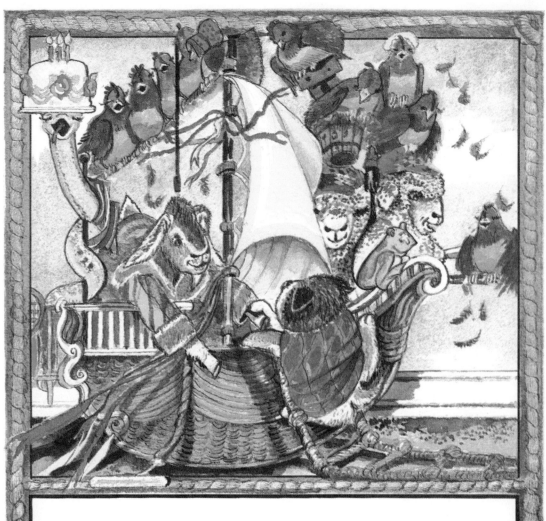

"Hop in," said the hens.

This is your floor.

We can make room for just one more.

So ten red hens, a snake with a cake,
two blue sheep,
a goat with a coat, and a pup . . .

. . . WENT UP!